EGMONT
We bring stories to life

First published in Great Britain in 2020 by Egmont UK Limited
2 Minster Court, 10th floor, London EC3R 7BB
www.egmont.co.uk

Written by Laura Jackson. Designed by Martin Aggett.
Cover illustration by Vic Blankenbaker.
Based on episode written by Michael White.

 Thomas the Tank Engine & Friends™

HiT entertainment   **CREATED BY BRITT ALLCROFT**

ISBN 978 0 7555 0043 7
71364/001

Printed in Great Britain

Thomas and the Royal Engine

This is a story about Thomas, and the day he had to take The Fat Controller on a very special journey ...

It was a sunny morning on Sodor. Thomas the Tank Engine was getting ready for a Very Important job. He was taking The Fat Controller to London to meet the Queen.

Thomas' cab had been swept clean, his firebox was full of coal and he had been scrubbed until he was the **shiniest** engine on Sodor.

Peep! Peep!
Thomas whooshed proudly down the
track to pick up The Fat Controller.
Next stop, London!

Clickerty-clack, clickerty-clack.

"Are you sure this is the way to London, Thomas?"
The Fat Controller called out of the window.

"Hmm, I think so ..." said Thomas.
But he couldn't quite remember.

The track quickly became dark and overgrown. Branches scratched at Thomas' paintwork.

"*Maybe I should have taken the other line ...*" thought Thomas.

He **puffed** and **chuffed** as fast as he could go. Broken branches fell all over poor Thomas. Then he spotted the Main Line ahead.

Phew! They were back on track.

Further down the line, a big tender engine was steaming up behind Thomas. The engine didn't see the muddy puddle on the tracks ahead.

She was chuffing **faster** and **faster** and **faster**. She wasn't going to slow down …

SPLASH!

Muddy water sploshed all over Thomas and The Fat Controller!

Thomas stopped at the next station. *"Go and find a Washdown, Thomas,"* said The Fat Controller. *"Hurry!"*

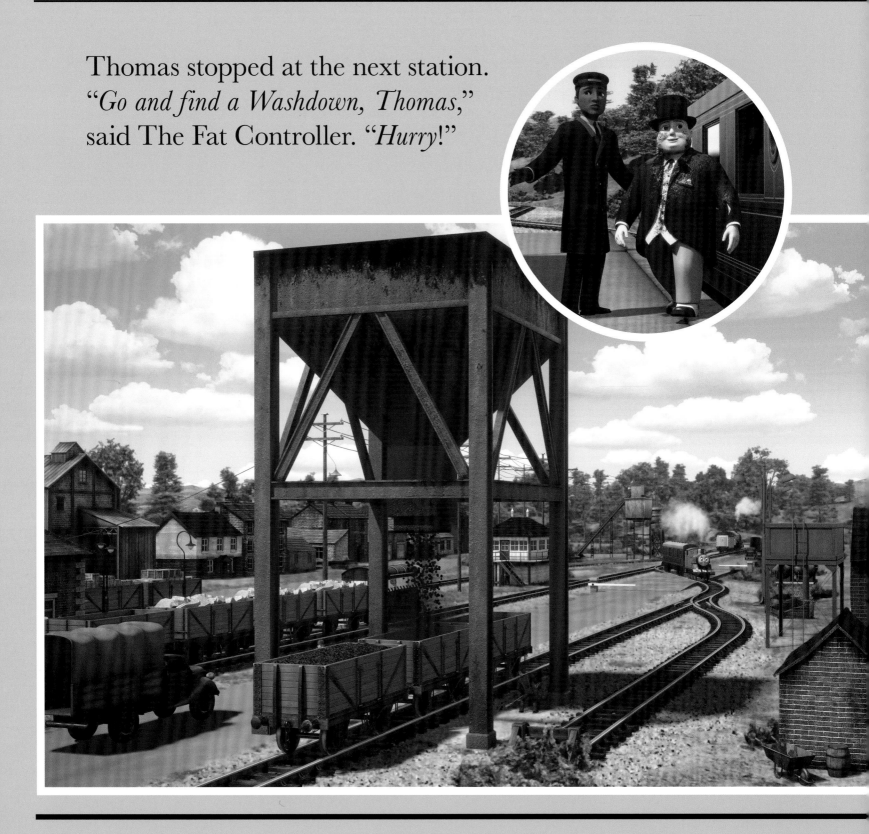

Somebody else was also looking for the Washdown that day. It was the big tender engine. She was in such a hurry, she shunted Thomas into some coal trucks.

Puff! Black dust covered Thomas from funnel to footplate.

"*Sorry!*" said the engine.
"*My name is Duchess …
Duchess of Loughborough.*"

"*Mine is Thomas … of Sodor!*"
giggled Thomas.

"*Oh, there's so much to do!*" gasped
Duchess. "*And I have to pick up
some Very Important passengers …*"

Thomas kindly let Duchess get
cleaned up first. But the workers
used all of the water in the tank.
There was no water to clean
Thomas.

Thomas was **dirtier** than ever. And there was only one hour left to get to London.

In a panic, The Fat Controller left the fireman behind at the station. Now there was nobody to shovel coal into Thomas' firebox. Thomas just couldn't pick up speed.

"Right, I'll be your fireman," The Fat Controller called out. *"You can't run a railway without getting your hands dirty!"*

Whirr, whirr, whirr! Thomas' wheels sped along the track.

"*London, here we come!*" he sang out.

Then up ahead, Thomas noticed somebody on the line. It was Duchess.

"*My safety valve has burst, Thomas!*" said Duchess. "*Now my Very Important passengers will be late to London.*"

Thomas couldn't leave a friend in trouble. Even if he was running late for the Queen! He offered to push Duchess and her carriages all the way to London.

He heaved and pushed and puffed with all his might.

"Thank you, Thomas of Sodor!" called out Duchess.

When Thomas pulled into Victoria Station, he was tired and dirty. But he had made it to London on time!

The Fat Controller was busy looking at something on the platform. There was a royal crown on Duchess' buffer. And somebody Very Important was stepping out of her carriages …

… the Queen!

Thomas had rescued the Royal Train!

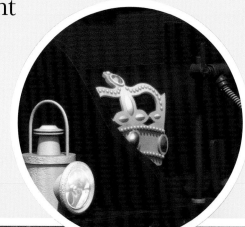

"*Sir Topham Hat*," smiled the Queen. "*Your railway is known for helping those in need.*"

"*They made sure we got here on time, Ma'am,*" Duchess told the Queen.

The Queen handed The Fat Controller a very special railway award.

"*Oh, thank you, Your Majesty,*" said The Fat Controller.

The Queen turned to Thomas and gave him a colourful medal.

"And gallant Thomas," said the Queen. *"This is for helping an engine in need and for being a Royally Useful Engine."*

Thomas **beamed** from boiler to buffer. He may not have been the shiniest engine on the tracks that day, but he was certainly the most useful.

About the Author

The Reverend W. Awdry was the creator of 26 little books about Thomas and his famous engine friends, the first being published in 1945.

The stories came about when the Reverend's two-year-old son Christopher was ill in bed with the measles. Awdry invented stories to amuse him, which Christopher then asked to hear time and time again.

And now for 75 years, children all around the world have been asking to hear these stories about Thomas, Edward, Gordon, James and the many other Really Useful Engines.

THE THREE RAILWAY ENGINES, *first published in 1945.*

The Reverend Awdry with some of his readers at a model railway exhibition.